D1360735

·Island Child·

by LISA WALLIS
illustrated by DEBORAH HAEFFELE

LODESTAR BOOKS
Dutton *New York*

The artist thanks Robert Gambee for graciously
permitting his book *Nantucket Island*
(W.W. Norton & Co., New York, NY, 1986)
to be used as visual reference in the creation of
several illustrations for *Island Child*.

Library of Congress Cataloging-in-Publication Data

Wallis, Lisa.

Island child/by Lisa Wallis; illustrated by Deborah Haeffele.
p. cm.
Summary: A child on an island goes for bike rides, crunches
icicles, and searches for sea glass on the shore.
ISBN 0-525-67324-5
[1. Islands—Fiction.] I. Haeffele, Deborah, ill. II. Title.
PZ7.W15937Is 1991
[E]—dc20
90-6184
CIP
AC

Published in the United States by Lodestar Books,
an affiliate of Dutton Children's Books,
a division of Penguin Books USA Inc.
375 Hudson Street, New York, New York 10014

Published simultaneously in Canada by
McClelland & Stewart, Toronto

Editor: Virginia Buckley
Designer: Marilyn Granald

Printed in Hong Kong
First Edition
10 9 8 7 6 5 4 3 2 1

for Cassie and Andrew

L. W.

with love to Sherry, Charlene, and Madeleine

D. H.

When I was a child on the island
I searched for pieces of colored sea glass
and shell-pink stones
on the shore near my home.

When I was a child on the island
I climbed the rocks
around the lighthouse
to watch for the ferry.
Sometimes I knew a passenger,
and sometimes I did not.
But I always waved.

When I was a child on the island
I walked with my family to the wharf
early each Sunday evening.
We listened to music at the bandstand
and ate bright red ropes of licorice
that stuck to our teeth.

Later, we wandered into the fish market
to gaze at black-green lobsters
in their darkened tanks.

When I was a child on the island
I played flashlight tag
with my sisters and brothers
and our friends next door.
Hiding along the Indian trail
beyond the old stone wall,
we hushed and *shsh*ed and
called out each other's names
in the warm summer air.
Crouching there, we waited
for the first beam of light
as it flashed in the night
rounding the far corner of our house.

When I was a child on the island
I climbed the wooden pole
that rose from the ground at a slant
to the top of the old mill.

A short way up I would stop and sit,
then swing my legs on either side.
With the wind in my face,
blowing my hair behind me,
I imagined I was a sea captain
forging home
through foaming waves.

When I was a child on the island
I pedaled out of town
toward the sea where the seals are.

On my way, I passed a small farm
with chickens and rocking chairs.
I could see cucumbers and strawberries
growing in a garden,
and clumps of peach and
yellow marigolds
by the porch stairs.
Once, a basket of lumpy
apples sat in the road
and I wondered what
it was doing there
as I steered my way past.

When I was a child on the island
I lay on my back in the forest;
the honey-colored pine
needles my mattress,
the warmth from
the sun my blanket.

I would close my eyes,
then listen
to the trees creaking in the
afternoon breeze,
their penny-brown cones
dropping to the ground
with light thumps.

Sparrows, juncos, and ruby-crowned kinglets
trilled and babbled and sang
while mice scurried about,
collecting seeds in the underbrush.

Sometimes I would hear a shout from the bike path
near my secret hiding place,
a chain saw in the distance
starting, stopping,
or the cry from one lonely gull overhead.

When I was a child on the island
I slipped my way over
the frozen cobblestones
of Main Street,
crunching on icicles that
stuck to my mittens
and sparkling chunks
of crusted snow.

Filling my mouth with cold,
I trudged to the corner bookstore
and traced my name on
its frosted windows.
Later in the week,
I could still see the letters
clearly etched on the icy panes.

When I was a child on the island
I rode my bicycle
to the oldest part of the graveyard
on foggy afternoons.

My friends and I whispered ghost stories
and made stone rubbings
of our favorite names and dates.

When I was a child on the island
I picked blackberries in the
hot August sun,
filling my pail to the rim
for making jam
and just plain eating.

When I was a child on the island
I painted one-eyed purple whales
and poppy-orange windmills
on wide, flat rocks
to sell at the sidewalk art show.

People gathered from all around,
pushing bikes and babies
past the sailboats in the harbor.

When I was a child on the island
I raced with my sisters
to the top of the highest dune.

Standing tall in the breeze,
we tasted the salt on our skin.
We jumped, then,
and laughing,
shook sand from our bathing suits.

When I was a child on the island
I counted fireflies and stars
outside my window,
and the number of times
the church bells chimed,
just in case it really wasn't my bedtime.

Snuggling under the covers
I imagined being a grown-up.
I would live on the island,
of course,
with children and a house
and roses all about.

And . . .
Perhaps I would climb the pole to the mill,
crunch icicles still,
and search for sea glass on the shore near my home.